For Oliver & Oliver
From Philip & Erin

Text copyright © 2015 by Philip C. Stead
Illustrations copyright © 2015 by Erin E. Stead
A Neal Porter Book
Published by Roaring Brook Press
Roaring Brook Press is a division of Holtzbrinck Publishing Holdings Limited Partnership
175 Fifth Avenue, New York, New York 10010
The art for this book was made using carbon transfer printing, egg tempera, and charcoal.
mackids.com

Library of Congress Cataloging-in-Publication Data

Stead, Philip Christian.
　Lenny & Lucy / written by Philip C. Stead ; illustrated by Erin E. Stead.
　　p. cm.
"A Neal Porter Book."
　Summary: «A picture book about moving to a new house and making new
friends —Provided by publisher.
　ISBN 978-1-59643-932-0 (hardback)
　[1. Moving, Household—Fiction. 2. Friendship—Fiction.] I. Stead, Erin E.,
illustrator. II. Title. III. Title: Lenny and Lucy.

PZ7.S808566Le 2015
[E]—dc23
　　　　　　　　　　　　　　　　　　　　2015001166

Roaring Brook Press books may be purchased for business or promotional use. For information
on bulk purchases please contact Macmillan Corporate and Premium Sales Department
at (800) 221-7945 x5442 or by email at specialmarkets@macmillan.com.

First edition 2015
Book design by Philip C. Stead
Printed in China by RR Donnelley Asia Printing Solutions Ltd., Dongguan City, Guangdong Province

1　3　5　7　9　10　8　6　4　2

• LENNY & LUCY •

Written by PHILIP C. STEAD   Illustrated by ERIN E. STEAD

 A NEAL PORTER BOOK • ROARING BROOK PRESS • NEW YORK

WINDING ALONG A BUMPY ROAD,

through the dark unfriendly woods, Peter said,
"I think this is a terrible idea."

And when they'd finally left the woods and stood safely on the other side of the wooden bridge, Peter said, "This house is not as good as our old house. I want to go back."

But no one heard except for Harold—who was only a dog and couldn't do much about it (even though he wanted to).

Harold was a good dog.

At night Peter and Harold looked from the upstairs window, past the wooden bridge, out to the dark woods. Terrible things hid in the trees. Neither Peter nor Harold slept at all.

So the next day Peter made a tall pile of pillows. And after they'd toppled the pile six times Peter ran inside to find just the right blankets. He stitched and sewed and wrapped the pile up, tying it shut with string. He pushed and pulled and kneaded the wrapped-up pillows like dough.

And when he was done he named it Lenny, Guardian of the Bridge.

"Lenny will guard the bridge," said Peter, "and keep the dark woods on the other side where they belong."

Harold wagged his tail.

Peter and Harold watched from the upstairs window.
They felt safe knowing that Lenny was there. He guarded
the bridge—silently, patiently, but with no one to keep
him company.

"Do you think Lenny is lonely?" asked Peter.

Then they worried about Lenny and his loneliness.

And no one slept at all.

So the next day Peter brought breakfast to Lenny—toast and jam and a glass of milk. Then Peter gathered all the leaves on the ground and made a tall pile. And after they'd leapt into the pile seven times Peter ran inside to find just the right blankets. He pushed and pulled and kneaded the wrapped-up leaves like dough.

When he was done he named her Lucy.
And Lucy was a good friend to Lenny.

Everyone slept. And the dark woods stayed on the other side
of the bridge (where they belonged).

The next day Peter, Harold, Lenny, and Lucy played a game of marbles. Harold was champion, everyone agreed. For lunch they ate vegetable soup, and after soup Peter began a collection of rocks.

The others sat awhile, watching the woods and wondering about the things they couldn't see.

"Have you ever seen an owl?" asked Millie.

Millie lived next door. She had binoculars that everyone could share (and a bag of marshmallows, too).

"No," said Peter, "I have never seen an owl."
Harold hadn't either.

So Peter, Harold, Lenny, Lucy, and Millie sat together, watching out for interesting things.